# Colin the Campervan

First Published in the UK March 2015 by FBS Publishing Ltd.
22 Dereham Road, Thetford,
Norfolk. IP25 6ER

ISBN: 978-0-9932043-1-9

Cover Design and Illustrations by Owen Claxton
Text Edited by Alasdair McKenzie
Typesetting by Scott Burditt

Paper stock used is natural, recyclable and made from wood grown in sustainable
forests. The manufacturing processes conform to environmental regulations.

# Colin the Campervan

## By Timothy Bentinck

Illustrated by Owen Claxton

Fabulous BookS

www.fbs-publishing.co.uk

# Dedication

*To the memory of wonderful times with SGF 800V,
both alone and with my family. I grew up to the
sound of a Beetle engine; my sons Will and Jasper
have that same flat-four growl in their childhood.*

*Also in memory of my dear friend Peter
Ackerman, who died too young, and fond
memories of surfing together in Biarritz in VJB
228J, a Type One with sunshine roof.*

*Every VW campervan has tales to tell.*

# CONTENTS

# CHAPTER ONE
## ANDY

Colin was cold. He hadn't been driven for nearly two weeks, and now it had started to snow. His windows were frosted up, his door catches were frozen, the oil in his engine was getting hard with cold and his tyres were like ice blocks around his wheels. The water that had seeped into his cavities through the rust holes in his body had frozen solid, and he was wrapped in a freezing blanket of ice. Colin was not a happy camper.

His owner had never taken him camping. He was a plumber who had never done anything nice with Colin, had never spoken a kind word, but shouted and swore at him and kicked him when he wouldn't start. When the plumber had bought him five years before, he had taken out most of Colin's insides, leaving just the cupboards to carry his plumbing tools. Colin carried sinks, baths, bidets and boilers all around the town. His owner was a terrible driver who sometimes got drunk, and then Colin would drive into things, like lamp posts and other cars. No one liked him; he was dirty, battered and rusty. He smelt of oil and exhaust. His silencer had a hole in it, so he sounded as loud as a racing car, but because his owner never had him serviced, he was terribly slow, and got in the way of all the other traffic. Then they hooted at him and called him names, and Colin got sad and thought about the old days.

He remembered being a brand new campervan, standing proud in the London showroom, his paintwork gleaming, his chrome bumpers and door handles shining like the richest silver. He was the prize in a national competition, the first of the Type Twos, and people came from far and wide to admire him, and hope that they would be the lucky winner. His huge side door stood open, showing the gawping public his magnificent insides. He was beautiful. He had a carpet, a table, curtains, a fridge, a cooker and a sink with running water. He had the latest stereo cassette/radio with four speakers. The back seat turned into a double bed, and in the upraised roof were two bunks for children. A large four-man tent was attached to his side. The showroom display was finished off with sun loungers and an outdoor table and chairs, with parasol. It was at that table that the documents were signed that turned him over to the competition winner: Andy, his first, and up to now his only, friend.

Andy was a student from Woollahra in Sydney, doing a postgraduate course in Computer Science at the University of London. He didn't have much money, so he parked Colin in the University car park and lived in him, saving himself a fortune on rent. With the money he saved, he and his friends would take Colin on camping trips to Scotland and Wales. Once, they even went across the sea to France, and Colin had to put on yellow sunglasses and drive on the wrong side of the road. One day he forgot, and a French car left a long scratch down his side; both he and Andy took greater care after that. He'd loved it in France and couldn't wait for Andy to take him back there, but as the years went by, the camping trips were fewer and fewer as Andy struggled to make ends meet, until finally he didn't even have enough money for Colin's petrol, and he just used him to sleep in, stuck in the University car park.

Sometimes Andy would sit in the driver's seat and start the engine, and Colin's hopes would soar, as he thought they were off again on some new adventure, but Andy was just charging the batteries so that the inside lights would work, and after a while, he'd pat Colin's dashboard, say 'Sorry, chum,' and turn the engine off, and Colin would stay where he was. When Andy left college, he didn't have enough money to return to Australia and he couldn't find any work either, so he and Colin drifted round the countryside, stopping wherever Andy could find some casual labour to pay for food and enough petrol to get to the next town. Though these were not the happy days of old, at least they were out on the road together, and Colin felt he was doing what he was built for. He only wished that Andy wasn't so sad and lonely.

Eventually, Andy couldn't afford to keep him any longer and put an advert in a local paper. Lots of people came to see him, but Colin was no longer the shiny new camper he used to be. He'd been outside for six years, and recently Andy hadn't been able to look after him properly. The scratch he'd got in France hadn't been repainted, the rust had got in, and some of his paint was peeling off. The furniture inside was battered and worn from continuous living, and the engine was tired and noisy from neglect. Nobody bought him.

Andy tried again, this time asking for less money, and finally he was sold. There were tears in Andy's eyes as he said goodbye to his old friend. He'd been so happy when he'd won the competition, but now all his high hopes for the future had ended like this.

Colin was miserable and frightened. Miserable to be leaving the only person he knew, and frightened of his future which lay in the charge of one man— his new owner.

He remembered being a brand new campervan,
standing proud in the London showroom ...

# CHAPTER TWO
## The Plumber

His new owner's name was Colin too—Colin Hardy, and all he'd wanted from this camper was the number plate—COL 1N. He drove Colin to his farm in Yorkshire and put the plates on his brand new hot hatchback, showing off to his friends and telling them how clever he'd been, finding the registration on 'that grotty old van'. Colin was put in a barn—jacked up on bricks, his wheels taken off—and covered in a dust sheet. Colin felt as if he'd died; he couldn't move and he couldn't see. He had no friends, no name and no hope. Colin was the saddest van in the world.

He spent seven years in that barn. During that time his rust got worse, his paint peeled some more and the rubber seals in his engine dried up and started to perish. The dust sheet rotted and fell off, and no one bothered to replace it. A window had been left slightly open, and moths and other insects had crept inside and eaten away at his carpets, curtains and upholstery. Woodworm had got into his cupboards and wasps had built a nest in his fridge. Colin was being eaten alive.

One day, a plumber arrived to clear out the farm's drains. One of the manholes for the drains was right below where Colin was parked, so his wheels were found, and he was let down off the bricks and rolled out of the barn while the plumber got on with his work. Just having his wheels on again and standing in the sunlight made Colin feel wonderful, but he was so frightened of being put back inside for another seven years that when the plumber made an offer to buy him, which was accepted, Colin felt a rush of warmth and gratitude towards this man who had saved him from a slow decline to the scrapyard. His gratitude was misplaced, as Colin soon began to realise.

Everything started to go wrong with him. The oil seals that had dried up over the years began to leak oil everywhere. His tyres had perished and often went flat. The battery was old and wouldn't turn the starter motor, so Colin hardly ever got going without a push or a jump-start from the neighbour's Sierra. The plumber sometimes took him to a garage where they treated him terribly and did just enough work to keep him on the road, but his heater didn't work, and nor did his wipers or his washers or his stereo or a dozen other things.

And here he was, dying of cold, dreaming dreams of past adventures, while the present held him in its icy grip.

During that time his rust got worse, his paint
peeled some more and the rubber seals in his engine
dried up and started to perish.

# CHAPTER THREE
## Hope

It was snowing again. It had piled itself high on Colin's spare wheel, and his wipers held a thick duvet of snow on his windscreen. His street was not a busy one, but there was a regular passing of cars; Colin was jealous of every one of them. Hot engines, hot insides, quiet exhausts—as they cruised by slowly on the snow, he could hardly hear them.

Through the falling flakes, he saw one of them slow down, stop, and reverse back to Colin's forecourt. Its door opened and out stepped a figure that made his engine turn over. It was Andy. Had he recognised him? He walked up to Colin, bent down and rubbed the snow off his number plate. He stood up, looking puzzled, looked at the number plate again and shook his head, then turned and walked away. Colin was in a panic. 'It's me! It's me! You must recognise me, you must!' he implored, but Andy was back at his car and opening the door. He spoke to someone inside and shook his head once more. He started to get back into his car. Desperately, Colin summoned up all his strength to power the only thing he had left that still worked— the horn. With everything he had, he blew.

There was a pathetic gurgling sound, and Colin knew he'd lost. But Andy stopped, and turned, and looked at Colin once again. Then he strode across the pavement and walked around him. He scraped more snow off Colin's side where the wind had turned the snow to ice, and there he saw the scratch, the scratch he'd made in France on the wrong side of the road.

'Colin,' said Andy quietly, 'it's you.'

It was. He'd found his friend.

He scraped more snow off Colin's side where the
wind had turned the snow to ice, there he saw the
scratch, the scratch he'd made in France ...

## CHAPTER FOUR
### Reunited

'Only too pleased to be rid of the old wreck,' the plumber said. He'd been trying to sell Colin for months, but nobody would take him. He was amazed at how much Andy had paid, and glad to see the back of the rusty old camper.

Andy could afford him. He'd finally got a job with a computer company, stayed in England, bought a house and got married. His wife's name was Susan and they had two children, Billy, 10 and James, 6. Andy and Susan had met at work, where he designed and wrote in-car computer systems and she was part of a team that put microchips in things that had never had microchips in them before, like a table that sensed the height of the people sitting at it, and adjusted its height accordingly, and waste-paper baskets that emptied themselves when they were full. They weren't rich, but they certainly weren't poor, and when Andy saw what had happened to Colin, he knew what he had to do.

Colin was sent to a body shop. This was no

ordinary garage, but a team of specialists who only dealt with Type Two campers. He was welcomed with open arms. His advanced state of decay was seen as a challenge, and within hours, he had been stripped down to almost nothing. They took out his seats and cupboards, they took out his engine, and they took off his wheels, his doors and his pop-up roof. They stripped out his wiring, they cut off his rust, they burned off his paint and finally, they took out his mouldy old curtains.

When they'd finished he was just a shell, but he was still Colin and he felt grand. When he went to sleep that night in the warm workshop, he couldn't wait for the next morning. He was going to be rebuilt!

The welder was first.

# CHAPTER FIVE
## Rebuilt

The welder was first. He welded up Colin's underside and jacking points. He fitted new panels and welded them on. Colin was blinded by showers of sparks as the welder made him stronger and stronger. Andy arrived with two new batteries and began to wire him up again from scratch. The other mechanics started work. They fitted new doors, racing tyres, sporty seats and a brand new two and a half litre turbocharged Porsche engine with racing clutch. Susan and the children arrived with a new pop up roof, but it was different to his old one; it was thicker, longer and wider, and it had wires trailing from it, which were carefully connected to Andy's new electrical system. Slowly, the new Colin took shape.

Carefully, layer after layer of dove blue paint was sprayed on and baked. His undersides were sealed, his bumpers replaced, and his new spare tyre was bolted to his nose. They fitted carpets and cupboards, cooker and fridge, beds and a table, toilet and shower, all to Andy and Susan's careful specifications. They fitted a five Terabyte media system, with 14 speakers and five screens. They fitted an ingenious alarm, central locking, wireless broadband Internet access, air conditioning, central heating and a whole load of computerised gadgets that completely baffled Colin. They were all controlled by a central Artificial Intelligence computer that, using the built-in microphones and speakers, could understand and reply to human speech. As soon as this computer was installed Colin tapped into it, as this thing too was now part of his body. He and the computer became as one, and he realised he now had the power to actually speak to people. The computer, which had been built in France and was called Ma Cyve Ardisque, was only too happy. It'd been expecting to have to run everything itself, and having Colin make the decisions meant it could get on with what it was best at—numbers.

Finally, and for Colin this was the best moment of all, they hung up his new curtains.

He was ready.

Colin had never been so happy. He felt as if he were the king of the road. Instead of hooting, cars would slow down to admire him. Other vans waved and flashed their lights in envy and appreciation. He didn't get in anyone's way now—in fact, his new engine made him one of the fastest things on four wheels, and Andy never tired of showing off Colin's acceleration to flashy sports cars and arrogant road hogs in executive saloons.

Andy had always talked to Colin. When it was just the two of them and Colin had been his only friend, Andy had often wished that Colin could talk back to him. Now he could. His new computer system took the place of all Colin's old switches and dials. Whatever they wanted, they asked for, and Colin would answer their requests with a friendly 'OK Andy, or 'It's my pleasure, Sue.' Billy and James loved Colin. Most of the gadgets that Andy and Susan had installed were for them. Nothing in the back of the van was quite as it seemed. If Billy said, 'Games please, Colin!' the table top flipped over and became a computer console. It had all the latest games, and a few that Andy had written especially for them. If they tired of the games, the screen was also a TV monitor and all their favourite films were stored on Colin's computer. Colin loved the TV, particularly detective stories with car chases. He was dying to find out how fast he could really go with his new engine, and watched with longing as powerful cars tore recklessly through heavily built-up areas.

Hidden waterproof loudspeakers fitted just below Colin's front bumper were also connected to the computer. With a few simple commands, Billy or James could blast cars in front with a huge range of digital recordings: steam trains, stampeding buffalo, police sirens, rock music, football crowds or even their own voices. Whichever they chose, they were very, very loud, and on their first test run, a week away in the Welsh mountains, Andy had had to stop the boys using it after a little old lady in a Mini had been attacked by a low-flying jet and nearly died of fright.

The boys thought that Colin was the best thing in the world, but for Colin it was even more wonderful. He had found himself. This was who he was meant to be. The weeks spent building him in the factory at Wolfsburg, the final kitting out at the Karmann coachbuilding works, then the refit, the total rebuilding of his entire being, the endless testing, Andy getting terribly cross because he couldn't get his roof to work ... A van can get confused, and Colin had begun to question what he was really meant for. Now, with this family, on this trip, he understood.

Apart from the roof being fixed, there was only one thing left that had to be done. He had to find something that had been taken from him, and there wasn't a day that went by when that he didn't remember its loss—his number plate, for without his number plate he had no name. He wasn't COL 1N now, he was KU06 TOS and he hated it, but somewhere deep inside him, the hope still burned that one day, somewhere, he would find his name again.

It was the summer holidays, and Andy suggested they take Colin back to France, to test out the new features, explore Andy's old haunts and have some new adventures.

'Can we take the surfboards?' asked Billy.

'And the bikes?' said James.

'And the bathroom?' laughed Sue.

'Yup, they're all provided for. He's ready,' answered Andy, and he took them outside. Colin was standing on the forecourt in front of the garage.

'Colin,' said Andy.

'Yes, Andy?' Colin replied.

'Please convert.'

'No sweat.'

A moment passed. Then the most extraordinary thing happened. The deep roof that had been added in the early days of Colin's restoration started to glow, then it started to hum, then with a sort of drrrrrr - CHUNGK!! it detached itself from the top of the van and folded itself outwards until it was like a deep awning, the same length and width as Colin, sheltering his side entrance. There was a ZSCHOOOOOF!! and from the free sides of the roof dropped three venetian blinds, effectively forming a room with walls that could be opened or closed, lifted or dropped, depending on the weather and the time of day.

A groundsheet and carpet fell next, then a table, chairs and two bunks unfolded themselves and dropped into position.

'That's amazing!' Billy gasped. 'But why has it got venetian blinds? Aren't they a little bit, you know, flimsy?'

Andy went into the garage and returned with a shovel. He smashed at the blinds five or six times as hard as he could and made no impact whatsoever. Not even a scratch. He turned to the others.

'Kevlar, he announced. 'The strongest, lightest material in the world, developed for spacecraft. You won't get through that.'

He leaned triumphantly on his shovel, which broke, and sent him sprawling into the blinds. A hydraulic pipe in the roof, which had been weakened by the blows of the shovel, finally came loose and sprayed high pressure hydraulic fluid all over him, covering him in greasy goo.

'Malfunction', announced Colin. 'Voice control lost. Please go to manual.'

'Go on,' said Sue, laughing, 'switch him off then go inside and get cleaned up.'

'No need,' spluttered Andy as he got to his feet and pulled out of his sodden pocket a miniature remote control unit. 'I told you, it's all provided for.'

He pressed a button and the spray suddenly stopped, then he pressed another and a door-sized portion of one of the blinds shot up into the roof. They followed him inside. Another button. A flap between Colin's two rear windows opened and a shower unit folded out. Another flap lower down slid open, revealing the water controls. As a shower curtain descended around him, Andy turned to his family.

'This is also the loo,' he said as it fell out of the roof and hit him on the head.

By the following evening, Andy had fixed the little problems and they were ready to go. The bikes were slung on the special fold-out rack above the rear bumper, the surfboards were strapped to the roof, the papers, the milk and the cat had been seen to, and early next morning they set off for France.

**If Billy said, 'Games please, Colin!' the table top
flipped over and became a computer console.**

# CHAPTER SIX
## The Ferry

Colin had never liked ships. He wanted to be up on deck with the others, watching the seagulls and seeing the white cliffs disappear into the sea mist. But he couldn't, as he was stuck down in the noisy, smelly car deck, with his yellow sunglasses on, trapped between an enormous Belgian juggernaut and a German tourist coach. Well, he'd been in worse places, and he knew it wouldn't last too long, so he settled down to wait. He thought about some of those places, and remembered the bad old days, stuck up on bricks in the farm shed ... his treatment at the hands of the plumber ... As he drifted off to sleep, he began to think the car deck really wasn't such a bad place after all ...

A slight movement of his right-hand windscreen wiper woke him from his dreams. A man in naval uniform was standing directly in front of him, putting a large envelope under his windscreen. At least it looked like a naval uniform—it was difficult to see through his yellow sunglasses.

Colin was immediately suspicious. *You can't get a parking ticket on a ship; what on earth could it be? A blackmail threat? A letter bomb!?* Colin had seen films where that sort of thing happened all the time. He went to red alert—and all hell broke loose.

A noise like a wartime siren wound itself up to a deafening roar. A wild west steam train klaxon honked incessantly, a police siren approached from a distance and the Charge of the Light Brigade was apparently re-enacted on deck two of the *Pride of Dover*. Colin's sound effects were in overdrive. At the same time, the remote control unit in Andy's pocket started beeping urgently. He pulled it out, turned it off and looked at the small LCD screen. 'INTRUDER!' it said. Andy immediately ran off to find someone to let him down onto the car deck.

By the time he reached the deck, accompanied by the ship's security officer, everything was quiet.

'An alarm you say, sir? said the security officer scathingly. 'Seems like rather a quiet alarm, doesn't it?' He followed Andy towards where Colin was parked.

'It is now,' said Andy. 'It switches itself off once the intruder has been captured.'

'Captured?' The security officer started to laugh. 'We've only just got here.' However, when he saw what was stuck to the light blue camper van in front of him, he stopped laughing, and gawped. A fishing net made of spun Kevlar was hanging all around the van, and trapped so tightly inside it that he was unable to speak was a man by the name of Herbert Higgins, a kindly man with a deep love of Type Two camper vans. He was in a severe state of shock. He also just happened to be the Captain of the *Pride of Dover*. On the back of the envelope that he had left were the following words:

'If you ever want to sell this beautiful vehicle, please call 01677-297623 and ask for Herbert. I await your response with eager anticipation.'

A fishing net made of spun Kevlar was hanging all around the van, trapped so tightly inside it that he was unable to speak was Herbert Higgins ...

# CHAPTER SEVEN
## France

As they drove away from Calais in unaccustomed silence, Colin was not feeling very proud of himself. They had been lucky to get away with a caution, and Andy had had to dismantle the netting there and then, and leave it with Captain Higgins for a possible future police investigation. Andy gave Colin a stern talking-to, and it was only because the Captain was so impressed by Colin's amazing features that they had got off without anything worse happening to them.

That evening they stopped at a campsite, and Colin soon cheered up as he made the preparations for their first night together since his rebuilding. Up went the roof and down came the blinds, the furniture and the loo. When fully rigged he looked quite amazing, and soon a small crowd had gathered, all wanting to look inside and talk to Andy or Sue. It was fun for a while, but soon they began to tire of all the attention, and Andy suggested that the next night they find somewhere more isolated to stay.

'After all, we're completely self-sufficient, so we don't need all the facilities of a campsite. Let's go exploring!'

In the evening, Sue cooked them all a delicious meal in Colin's well appointed kitchen. They played boules with a French family who were camped next to them, and the boys didn't go to sleep till well after dark. They slept in two bunks that converted from the rear seats, while later in the evening Andy and Sue settled down in the folding double bed in the 'tent'.

The next morning they awoke to the sound of the sea lapping against the shore. Billy listened to it happily for a while; it was so soothing and gentle. With a start, he suddenly remembered that they were fifty miles inland, and leaped out of his bunk. He drew the curtains. No sea, just the campsite. What was going on?

'Good morning, boys!' said Colin, as James lifted a tousled head over the duvet. 'Don't you just love the sound of the sea? I recorded this at Dover. What do you think?' A wave crashed onto some rocks in the distance and a seagull cried overhead.

'I think,' said Billy grumpily, 'that you should stop giving people nasty shocks and make us all some breakfast.'

'Whatever you say,' said Colin, and a small hatch in the table slid open. Out of the hatch came two long plastic tubes which waved around in front of the boys' faces.

'For starters—Coke for Billy and Ribena for James. Am I right?' said Colin.

'You're right!' chorused the boys.

For the next few days they travelled south-west through the beautiful French countryside, through villages and towns, visiting cathedrals and museums (that was what the grown-ups wanted), to Disneyland Paris and go-karts, swimming pools and flumes (which was where they ended up) until, one hot July evening, in a pine forest north of Biarritz, they finally reached their goal, the sea.

That night they surfed in the moonlight, and as the waves crashed below him, Colin stood proudly on the dune above, his volume turned up to absolute maximum, answering the might of the Gallic sea with some serious British sound waves.

There was another couple surfing nearby, and earlier Colin had thought there was something familiar about the man, but his yellow sunglasses did tend to make things look rather odd—he really shouldn't have netted the ship's Captain - and he had dismissed the idea. Now, however, as they walked back from the sea towards him, Colin was sure that he had seen him somewhere before. He was also quite sure that he didn't like him. He looked towards their car. A Golf GTI. He moved his electric mirrors so that he could see the number plate, and his engine turned over so fast it started. 'COL 1N'. He couldn't believe it. It was Colin Hardy, the man who had left him in a farmyard for seven years, and more importantly, this was the man who had stolen his name. Colin went to yellow alert.

The family had finished surfing, and Sue and Andy were helping the boys get dry when the sound of an approaching helicopter made them all look up. The sound came closer, but they couldn't see anything. From the direction of the sound, the helicopter appeared to be landing almost directly on top of Colin. Suddenly, a blinding searchlight, apparently just above Colin's roof, pierced the darkness and picked out the red Golf GTI that was parked further down the dune.

'ATTENTION! ATTENTION!' A voice on a loudhailer could be heard coming from the hovering chopper, in English, but with a strong French accent. 'ZE OWNERS OF ZIS CAR, REGISTRATION NUMBER COL 1N ... I REPEAT, COL 1N ...' The voice seemed to be getting louder and more insistent. '... ARE UNDER ARREST. YOU WILL NOW BE APPREHENDED BY OUR GROUND UNIT, 'OO ARE DRESSED AS AN INNOCENT LOOKING ENGLISH FAMILY. DO NOT BE FOOLED, ZESE ARE ZE CRACK TROOPS OF ZE LEGENDARY FOREIGN LEGION. MESS WIZ ZEM AT YOUR PERIL.'

'It's Colin!' shouted Andy. 'He's gone mad! Come on.' And he rushed up the slope towards him.

Hardy and his girlfriend stood by their car, blinded by the searchlight and transfixed by the voice; it was like nothing they had ever heard before. But the light was getting dimmer.

'YOU ARE CHARGED WIZ 'AVING STOLEN ZE NUMBER PLATE OF A TYPE TWO VAN ...' The voice was getting fainter, and the helicopter appeared to be flying away. '... AND DISGUISING YOURSELF AS SOMEONE CALLED COLIN, WHICH IS AN HONOURABLE NAME, AND ONE ZAT YOU ARE **NOT WORZY TO BEAR!!!** ...' With this last cry, his voice faded out until it was barely a whisper. By the time Andy reached Colin, his batteries were completely flat—he'd drained all his power on the searchlight and the sea and helicopter effects, and now there was no power left to tell Andy what he had seen. Hardy desperately shoved his girlfriend into the car, and with engine racing and wheels spinning, they roared off into the warm French night.

Andy switched over to auxiliary power, started the engine and charged up the main batteries. Colin explained what had happened.

'Don't worry, Colin,' said Billy, giving his steering wheel a big hug, 'we all know it's you, even without your number plate. Anyway, I'll bet you anything you like that isn't the last we'll see of Mr Horrid Hardy.'

Now Billy was much too young to gamble, and anyway he didn't really have any proper money of his own (£2.36 in a Kiddi Klub savings account), but if he'd then bet a pound at a million to one, I can tell you now that Billy would have made a very great deal of money.

For Colin and his family, this was the beginning of many grand adventures, and the search for Colin Hardy would eventually take them all the way around the world.

I do hope that you'll come too …

Suddenly, a blinding searchlight, just above Colin's roof, pierced the darkness and picked out the red Golf that was parked further down the dune.

53

# Acknowledgements

To Judy, who had to put up with a left-hand drive machine whose windscreen froze from the inside, wouldn't start, and was impossible to drive. Colin is what we all dreamed of.

Look out for further adventures of ...

# COLIN
# THE
# CAMPERVAN

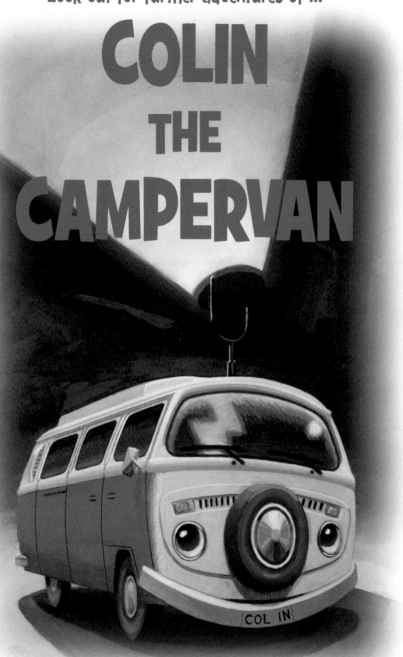

COL IN

www.fbs-publishing.co.uk

# About the Author

Best known as the voice of David Archer in the BBC Radio series, *The Archers*, Tim is also an accomplished stage, film, radio and television actor. From the swashbuckling Tom Lacey in the 80s series *By The Sword Divided* to starring with David Jason in 2012's *The Royal Bodyguard*, he has recently featured in *Twenty Twelve, The Politician's Husband, Eastenders, Lucan, Gangsta Granny* and plays the Home Secretary in the forthcoming BBC spy series, *The Game*. He starred as a bank robber in the short film *Locked Up* which won Best Short Film at the Lanzarote Film Festival in 2015.

He is a top voice artist and dubbing specialist, also an inventor, writer, travel journalist, computer programmer and musician. He went to Harrow, University of East Anglia, and trained as an actor at the Bristol Old Vic Theatre School.

In 2012 he won *Celebrity Mastermind*, (specialist subject Winnie the Pooh), beat Judith Keppel head-to-head in *Celebrity Eggheads*, then defeated Linford Christie and the tallest couple in Britain in *Pointless Celebrities*!

Besides broadcasting to 5 million listeners daily in *The Archers,* he is the voice of James Bond in *The World Is Not Enough* computer game and for 15 years was strangely familiar to Londoners as the voice of 'Mind The Gap' on the Piccadilly Line.

He lives in London with his wife Judy, a leading hat designer, and has two sons, Will, 30 and Jasper, 26.

Discover more at Tim's website:

www.bentinck.net

Lightning Source UK Ltd.
Milton Keynes UK
UKIC01n0158170615
253643UK00011B/59